Hello, Family Members,

Learning to read is one of the most important accomplishments of early childhood. **Hello Reader!** books are designed to help children become skilled readers who like to read. Beginning readers learn to read by remembering frequently used words like "the," "is," and "and"; by using phonics skills to decode new words; and by interpreting picture and text clues. These books provide both the stories children enjoy and the structure they need to read fluently and independently. Here are suggestions for helping your child *before*, *during*, and *after* reading:

Before

- Look at the cover and pictures and have your child predict what the story is about.
- Read the story to your child.
- Encourage your child to chime in with familiar words and phrases.
- Echo read with your child by reading a line first and having your child read it after you do.

During

- Have your child think about a word he or she does not recognize right away. Provide hints such as "Let's see if we know the sounds" and "Have we read other words like this one?"
- Encourage your child to use phonics skills to sound out new words.
- Provide the word for your child when more assistance is needed so that he or she does not struggle and the experience of reading with you is a positive one.
- Encourage your child to have fun by reading with a lot of expression . . . like an actor!

After

- Have your child keep lists of interesting and favorite words.
- Encourage your child to read the books over and over again. Have him or her read to brothers, sisters, grandparents, and even teddy bears. Repeated readings develop confidence in young readers.
- Talk about the stories. Ask and answer questions. Share ideas about the funniest and most interesting characters and events in the stories.

I do hope that you and your child enjoy this book.

Francie Alexander
Reading Specialist,
Scholastic's Learning Ventures

To all puppies, everywhere, including:
Willie, Wailin', Buddy, Mo-Mo, Bandit, Belle,
Roscoe, Spike, Kiva, Abe, Pumpkin, Amber, Teddy,
and yes, even Heidi.
— R.M.C.

ISBN 0-439-09856-4

Copyright © 2000 by Robin Michal Koontz.
All rights reserved. Published by Scholastic Inc.
SCHOLASTIC, HELLO READER, CARTWHEEL BOOKS and associated
logos are trademarks and/or registered trademarks of Scholastic Inc.

Library of Congress Cataloging-in-Publication Data
Koontz, Robin Michal.
    Why a dog? by A. Cat / by Robin Michal Koontz.
        p.   cm. — (Hello reader! Level 1)
    Summary: When A. Cat lists all the rhyming reasons that dogs are
not good pets, there is one final reason to have a dog for a friend.
    ISBN 0-439-09856-4
    [1. Cats—Fiction. 2. Dogs—Fiction. 3. Pets—Fiction. 4. Stories in
rhyme.] I. Title. II. Series.
PZ8.3.K8425Wh   2000
[E]—dc21
                                                            99-27025
                                                                CIP

12   11   10   9   8   7   6   5   4   0/0   01   02   03   04

Printed in the U.S.A.   24
First printing, January 2000

WHY A DOG?
by A. Cat

as told to:
Robin Michal Koontz

Hello Reader! — Level 1

SCHOLASTIC INC.
New York Toronto London Auckland Sydney
Mexico City New Delhi Hong Kong

Why a dog?
Dogs are bad!
Dogs do things
that make me mad...

Dogs slobber.

Dogs snore.

Dogs dump fur
all over the floor.

Dogs roll.

Dogs shake.

Dogs howl
and keep me awake.

Dogs whimper.

Dogs wag.

Dogs eat stuff
that make me gag.

Dogs dig.

Dogs chew.

Dogs throw up
in people's shoes.

Dogs sniff.

Dogs beg.

Dogs scratch
and lift their legs.

Dogs bark.

Dogs chase.

Dogs lick me
in the face.

Dogs pant.
Dogs fog.

You have me!
So why a dog?

Well, dogs are faithful.
Dogs defend.
I guess a dog
can be a friend.